The Haunted House of Buffin Street

You can read more stories about
the gang from Buffin Street by
collecting the rest of the series.

For complete list, look at
the back of the book.

The Haunted House of Buffin Street

Francesca Simon

Illustrated by Emily Bolam

Orion
Children's Books

The Haunted House Of Buffin Street first appeared in *Miaow Miaow Bow Wow*
first published in Great Britain in 2000
by Orion Children's Books
This edition first published in Great Britain in 2012
by Orion Children's Books
a division of the Orion Publishing Group Ltd
Orion House
5 Upper St Martin's Lane
London WC2H 9EA
An Hachette UK Company

1 3 5 7 9 10 8 6 4 2

A catalogue record for this book is available from the British Library.

ISBN 978 1 4440 0469 4

Printed in China

The Orion Publishing Group's policy is to use papers that are natural,
renewable and recyclable products made from wood grown in sustainable forests.
The logging and manufacturing processes are expected to conform
to the environmental regulations of the country of origin.

www.orionbooks.co.uk

For my mother-in-law,
Gwen Stamp

Woof

Fang

Miaow

Flick

on Buffin Street

Caw Caw

Do-Re-Mi

Miaow

Lola

Woof

Honey

Snuffle snuffle

Lily

Miaow

Kit

Bow wow

Prince

Rustle
rustle

Jogger

Growl

Sour Puss

Bow wow

Dizzy

Miaow

Millie

Squeak

Doris

Squeak

Boris

Miaow

Joey

Welcome to Buffin Street!

Come and join all the Buffin Street
dogs, cats, rabbits, puppies and parrots,
and find out what *really* goes on when
their people are out of sight…

"You're joking," said Honey.

"Would I joke about something
so awful?" said Fang.

"But it can't be true!"
said Honey. "I like it here.
I don't want to move."

"What we want doesn't matter," said Fang sadly. "They want to move and there's nothing we can do about it."

"But why move?" said Honey.

"They want a house with
a garden," said Fang.

"A garden?" said Honey,
perking up for a moment.
Then she sighed again.

"I'd rather stay in Buffin Street
with our little patio than have
a garden," she said.

Prince poked his nose
through the fence.
"Bad news, eh?" he said.

"The worst," said Fang.

"What about me?" said Prince.
"I don't want new neighbours. For all
I know the new ones might hate dogs.

Or worse, have a horrible
yappy dog themselves. Or..."
he groaned "...a cat."

"Nothing wrong with cats,"
said Millie, leaping down
the fire escape.

"Cats are purrrrfect,"
said Lola.

"Ha," said Prince, bristling.

"Stop it, you two," said Do-Re-Mi,
flying down from the window.

"The main thing is, how can we
keep Fang and Honey here?"

Everyone stood in silence.

"It's hopeless," said Fang.
"The new people are coming
tonight to look round one
last time and sign the papers.
It's too late."

"No it isn't," said Millie.
"I've got a plan that just might work."

Everyone stared at Millie. It wasn't
like her to have a plan.
"Well, let's hear it," said Fang.

Do-Re-Mi saw the new people walking down Buffin Street and squawked a warning.

"They're coming!" said Lola.

"Positions everyone!" said Millie.

Prince started howling.

"Awhooooo!
Awhooooo!"

Then Dizzy did too.

"Awhooooo!
Awhooooo!"

Then the Alley Cats
joined in.

"Miaow
Yow Yow!
Miaow
Yow Yow!"

"What a noisy street,"
said the woman.
"I had no idea," said the man,
ringing Fang's door bell.

The animals heard the door
open, and then footsteps
coming down the hall.

"Doris and Boris first!"
whispered Millie.

The mice skittered
across the room.

"Eeeee! Mice!"
squealed the woman.

"Disgusting!"
shouted the man.

"Go for it!" said Millie.

"Ooooooooooooooooooo!"
moaned Fang.
"Ooooooooooooooooooo!"
moaned Honey.

"Sssssssss!"

hissed Lola and Millie,
their swishing tails making
the curtains sway.

"Scraaaaaaatch!"
went Lily's sharp claws
on the wooden floor.

The people froze.

"What's that noise?" said the woman.

"I don't know," said the man.

"Oooooooooooooooooo!"
moaned Fang and Honey.

"I don't like this,"
said the woman.

"Ssssssssssssssssssssss," hissed
Lola and Millie, a little louder.

"Scraaaaaaatch!"
scraped Lily's claws.

Suddenly Do-Re-Mi swooped.

"Squawk! Squawk!
Squawk!
Go away!"
she screeched.

"Aaaahhhh!"

shrieked the people.

"The house is haunted!
Help!"

And they ran
screaming out
of the door.

"We did it!" cheered the animals.
"Three cheers for Millie!"
It was nothing, really," said Millie,
hanging her head shyly.

After this Fang and Honey's haunted
house became famous up and
down Buffin Street.
No one wanted to move there.
Which suited the animals just fine.

Miaow
follow me

Did you enjoy the animals' haunting of Buffin Street? Can you remember all the things that happened in the story?

What do Fang and Honey think is so awful?

Why do Fang and Honey's people want to move?

What is Prince worried about when he hears the news?

Why does Fang think it's too late to stop it from happening?

Who has an idea that just might work?

Who skitters across the floor and
frightens the people?

Who scratches her claws on the
wooden floor?

Why does no one want to move into Fang and Honey's house on Buffin Street any more?

For more adventures with the
Buffin Street Gang, look out for
the other books in the series.

Meet
the Gang

Yum Yum

Rampage in Prince's Garden

Jogger's Big Adventure

Miaow
Miaow
Bow Wow

Look
at Me

Look out for more Early Readers
by Francesca Simon and Emily Bolam

Runaway Duckling

Where Are My Lambs?

Billy the Kid Goes Wild

Barnyard Hullabaloo

Mish Mash Hash

Chicks Just Want To Have Fun

Moo Baa Baa Quack